Text and illustrations copyright © 2022 by Eva Montanari
Published by arrangement with Debbie Bibo Agency

Tundra Books, an imprint of Penguin Random House Canada Young Readers, a division of Penguin
Random House of Canada Limited

Library and Archives Canada Cataloguing in Publication

Title: What does little crocodile say : at the park / Eva Montanari.
Names: Montanari, Eva, 1977– author.
Identifiers: Canadiana (print) 20200381369 | Canadiana (ebook) 20200381423 | ISBN 9780735268159
   (hardcover) | ISBN 9780735268166 (EPUB)
Classification: LCC PZ7.M763 Wha 2021 | DDC j823/.92—dc23

Published simultaneously in the United States of America by Tundra Books of Northern
New York, an imprint of Penguin Random House Canada Young Readers, a division of Penguin
Random House of Canada Limited

Library of Congress Control Number: 2020949587

Edited by Samantha Swenson
Designed by Kate Sinclair and Orith Kolodny
Hand lettering by Eva Montanari
The artwork in this book was rendered in colored pencil and chalk pastel.

Printed in China

www.penguinrandomhouse.ca

1 2 3 4 5   25 24 23 22 21

Penguin
Random House
tundra | TUNDRA BOOKS

To Ruggero's grandparents
and to all grandparents.

WHAT DOES LITTLE CROCODILE SAY AT THE PARK?

Eva Montanari

tundra

THE BELL GOES
DING-DONG.

THE DANDELION
GOES PFFFF.

THE LIZARD
GOES SWISH.

THE PIGEONS GO
FLAP FLAP FLAP.

THE CHATTER
GOES CHITCHAT.

THE MERRY-GO-ROUND GOES...

TAKEN !

AND WHAT DOES
LITTLE CROCODILE SAY?

THE DUCK SAYS "QUACK!"

HAPPINESS GOES YIPPEE!

THE OWL SAYS
"HOO HOO."

THE DONKEY SAYS "HEE-HAW."

THE CHICK SAYS "PEEP PEEP."

THE FRIENDS SAY
"BYE-BYE!"

THE LULLABY

GOES ROCK-A-BYE-BABY...